OF WELTER AND WHIM
MIKE MAC

MIKE MAC

For my loving mother

THE WELTER

She kept sunsets in jars
And butterflies in her stomach
Yet listened to Motörhead
And sang along to Danzig

To count the rain
Was to know the ways I loved her

Unbeknownst
To many of most
I've seen a ghost

He appeared
In mirror
Before me clear

I gestured as such
And he did as much

With hesitation
We both spoke
Of deprecation

He assured me
I'd be fine
And I thanked him
For his time

Soulmates
We are not
But my love for her
Is as sure as the freckles on her face
And I know of no greater prerequisite
For such divinity

Alcohol
Woke the devil in him
Like a box car racer
Over a pothole
He became unbridled
Uproarious at the whisk
Of the most peevish trifle
He sought a kind of justice
For his feral belligerence
An anti-hero
Who didn't fight his demons
But joined them

I saw the devil
There in flesh
Order a whiskey
Barman's best
With eyes too wintry
For a summer's dress
She licked her lips
And sealed my hex

Unlike truth
Honesty is a paradox
Having never once left the cull
Of the revisionist mind

Grim the clock
That ticks nor tocks
Atop the tower
Wrick with wroth
Where hangs a fowler
Feet from knot
Strike every hour
It tolls a flock
To pick the prowler
Clean from rot

Grim the Clock

She
Had gone
I could no more
Outrun thoughts of her
Than I could outrun the rain
And I would have it no other way

The Devil strolled
    Through God's acre
        Counting tombstone tragedies
And took great joy
    In the sorrow bore
        By the mourning families
Then one day
    He saw a man
        Sobbing atop the leaves
Upon near sight
    He was startled to find
        It was he who wept on knees
Before a gravestone
    That read in part
        The Devil whom no one grieves

I
was unable to
dissuade my eyes from
her. She was extraordinary.
A serendipitous confluence of
quirk. An ethereal symphony of
vitality amidst the dull drone of
our doom. A windfall of cosmic
liberty in stark defiance of laws
deemed absolute. A chance
at chance. A rose upon
the moon.

He was hanged for treason
After a courtyard quarrel
Over imploring reason
And its corollary morals
While calling into question
The presiding laurels
Of God's jurisdiction
Over *sinful* mortals

Then I'll go
To the space between
Words and poetry
Where stars swirl
The fingers of those
Who swim the night's sea
And sandcastles
Wash ashore

My
Ribs
Are of
Wicker
They bend
And splinter
I wish they were
THICKER
Your embrace
Is bitter-
Sweet

Atop the iron gate
Of a decrepit manor
Perched a gargoyle
Mouthing a lantern
Yond tattered choremen
Plodded the grounds
Under watch of a warden
Ringed by ravenous hounds
Upon my pry
A tiny placard read:
If you can read this sign
You will soon be dead
Then fell the lantern
Upon my crown
Death became me
Now I chore the grounds
In fear of the warden
And his horde of hounds

The Manor

The
Rain
Danced
Drunk as
Moonshine
Off the tin roof

We are all the eye of our own storms

My
Love
Left me
Long ago
But I do not
Have the *heart*
To let her know

The homeless man vexed
Those around him
Wishing away his coins
At the foot of the fountain
A penny for your thoughts?
Broached a miss
Her tranquil blue eyes
Pierced pearlescent skin
As her lavish lips bosomed
Above a feminine chin
He accepted her offer
Under her one condition
It be kept in his coffer
And used with discretion
She returned everyday
Hearkening his woes
At cost of a coin
For each rue disclosed
As time progressed
His coffer brimmed
He went to a barber
For a proper trim
He bought a new suit
And built a new life
He purchased a ring
And asked her his wife
She whispered his ear
I'm glad you're alright
His cheek dropped a tear
As she rippled from sight

The Fountain

I could never lose someone
As much as I lost you

Starlight eyes
Of moonlight gorge
Tell me the story
Of your quiet sighs
Sequestered ties?
Recanted love?
Or is it merely
The moon above

Her
Words
Were curt,
Irate, and keen
Primed for print
In a rolled up magazine

How wroth I wallow
How grim my gloom
I howl in harrow
Pleading my exhume
In beseech of the hallow
Who damned my doom
To rap of the devil
Dancing on my tomb

Undead

Troubled soul
Do you not know
The winds will still blow
And the tides will still roll

I smolder in wane
I needn't remember
For I was once flame
Now only an ember

I
Wish
No more
To think of thee
For to dream of shore
One must admit the sea

She stood the forest lone
Lost to all bereaved
Rooted as if sown
Beneath the fallen leaves
Muttering in drone
I do so as I please
In a voice not her own
Just as the howls of the trees

The Forest Woman

I saw the devil
Dancing alone
Touting his sins
In gleeful gloat
I asked of him
(To be so bold)
Had he no burden
For which he bode
He sobered grim
Thumbing his nose
How petty the God
Who thorns the rose

She
Was both
Fire and flame
But never the same

I
Ran
From her
Rabid words
Into the dark forest
From which they came
Knowing she would
Never come back
For them
There

Oblique the callow
Heavy with horns
Mar of the hallow
Who damned you born

My casket
Will bear the corpses
Of a man and his remorses

Darkness fell
From sea to shore
For the heavens
Had shut its door
To those of whom
Had faith no more
Gleaming sea life
Took to soar
As once the stars
Had shone before
Opening anew
The sacred door

Doors

I killed you off in my last chapter
But I am unable to write you from my pages
For your blood still wets my pen

Mid the din
Of a fire spree
Stood akin
The devil in me
Lauding sin
In scorn of doxy
Imparting a grin
As I by proxy

The winds will rescind
And the rains will quell
The heavens will open
To an introspective hell
They'll forgive your sins
But never themselves

Heaven

She was a maniac; and I, crazy for her

Drum thunder
Crack lightning
The patter rains
A silver lining
To the creatures
Who've long seen
The night dream

I
Saw
Vultures
In her eyes
Circling overhead
I knew that I had died
When she left me for dead

Yes, we fare on
For kin do us bide
And the deeds
We have done
Ripple in reprise
But life is a lesson
In certain demise
As a universe
From nothing
Has nothing
To hide. You see,
Heaven and hell
Is merely lore
Aimed to impel
Tithes for war
A conjure
Of conspire by
Canting scribes
To weild hell's fire
'Gainst whom decried
The greed of empire
And a sect gone wry

He was big headed
And small minded
A walking contradiction
And a running joke

The Devil retorted
Oh, how lamb
For you to abhor
No bane of battle
Could null your war
You build your gallows
In sport of the poor
Beneath phallic steeples
That decry the 'whore'
Yet those who rally
Venture God's favor
While more as I
Welcome that wager

I tasted war on her lips
And saw peace in her eyes
'Twas a lovers kiss
But we still held our knives

Like oil to a flame
Her ink spill'd the page
Little fires in her name
Each a war she waged
'Gainst the umbral reign
Of an omnipotent sage
Whose cannon the blame
For a benighted age

Let There Be Light

I am not so godless
As to mistake her freckles for faults
Before the stars that placed them

Down
Poured the rain
On a stormful night
Upon harrow'd graves
Of the township's blight
Where mourned a crow
Of wont and name
Vowed their valor
Would be remained
She flew the weather
To history's doorstep
Sparing a feather
Lest we forget
Q
u
i
l
l

In the end
All that is dark
Will outlast the light
For mortal the day
And eternal the night

She could be found
Beyond the bounds
Of the hunting hounds
For she ran with the wolves

For her
Time stood still
On weak knees
And I
Fared no better

Be gone curs-ed fowl
Who perches my crux
Upon the harrow'd rows
Of Autumn's till
I beseech my repose
For I am of wisp n' wit
I am of fault n' frill
These shoes I fit
I will never fill

Scarecrow

Littering her floor
Lay crumpled pages
Like the dead flies
On the window sill
Each sinuate edge
A leg curling inwards

Outside
A butterfly, frantic
In the tattered web
As the ruin of confinement
So the trappings of favor
Her thoughts return
To the oak tree
At yard's end
Where her sin once hanged
In melancholy
Better to be found
Than seen

Trappings

THE WHIM

I let you walk all over me
But next time
I'm going to be a Lego

When my roommate sprays
Himself with Axe body spray
I wait for him to leave
And then walk through it

Easier on the bank

My love,
I want to write
Of the beauty of your eyes
And the looks that you give me
But you are cross-eyed
So I will speak instead
Of your large
Comforting hands

My days are usually usual
As chance would have it
Some days are unusual

I've said too much

Surrender
My vandalism verdict
To the chancellors of charm
So their vernacular
Is of lesser harm
Be sure of its stout
For I know my abouts
At the time of the crime
I was robbing a bank
After waiting in line

Alibi

Who thinks they're quick?
He said in dare
With a gun on his hip
And a wry in his glare
A man stood tall
With a bullet in his teeth
And proclaimed with gall
Let's take it to the street
They stepped outside
And faced each other
But could not decide
What rules would govern
One said ten count
The other said three
A third let out
An ardent plea
You'll settle no score
Stop this rattle
No greater burden bore
Than the bane of battle
The men agreed
And hung their necks
They drank whiskey
Then dueled the check

Her beautiful madness
Danced in my mind
With a final curtsy
Of humorous kind

If only truth had the endurance of gossip

I made the adult decision
To purchase a plastic Samurai sword
Because I know that a real one
Can be dangerous
Maturity creeps up on you

She whispered in my ear
I'm not wearing panties
I whispered back
Neither am I

I made her laugh and she said I was stupid
I've fancied myself an idiot ever since

Doctor
Come quickly
My spirit animal
Has bit me
The crystals
You gave me
Did nothing
To save me

Alternative
Medicine

In brush with my mortality
I promised greater purpose
But fell guilty to the formality
Of trite rhymes n' simple verses
To indemnify this banality
I became a one man circus
And inked my ass in rhapsody
In affront to panes of churches

Schismatic

I assure you my intentions are diabolical

I threw an orange at an apple tree
Hoping to knock an apple free
I missed and lost them both
Unfortunately
But what made me sad
Is that I had nowhere else to be

The last party I went to
Was a funeral
The guy was a klepto
Who took too many chances
Died in a freak volcano accident
His name was James Francis
The apple of my eye
Was hit by Cupid's arrow
She left me for another guy
Who drove a Camaro
The guy was a klepto
Who stole too many dances
Now that you mention it
His name was James Francis

Geese
Need cease
With the feces

Sured my inclination
To goad trapper's ware
For I seek to be strung
By the trap that ensnares
If only to acquaint
With a pardoner's air
Thee who unwittingly
Summoned my dare

I have an exorbitant literacy rate

I read you my poetry
And kiss your face in a new spot
After every word

Farewell men
You shall find me
In the bosom of heaven
The captain cocksure
As he walked the plank
With glee

M u t i n y

Kindly consider reviewing this book.
Thank you!